Diary of Tweaky
the Sparrow

A Fantasy Story

RAJENDRA NAIK

Contents

Chirpter 1

Right on the edge of the luxuriant thicket of Sugarcane field, there stands a Champa tree. Young children of humans, working in the field, often come to play in the shade under the Champa tree.

They look so harmless – not like the rapacious men and woman, dwarfed by the tall sugarcanes, wielding little axes to harvest the crop.

No one knows who planted the Champa tree but the older sparrows, like my own grandpa, never got tired of regaling young ones like me how it had been just a sugarcane field with this Champa tree and then came a cunning group of men to build a nest of their own, uncomfortably close to our Champa tree. It was fun, listening to the long drawl chirpy tone of the old Grandpa straining his eyes, in the crepuscular evening rays of the sun, to seek me out from the group of young sparrows.

My Ma, Grandpa's darling, was the least gullible of the lot. She was not to be amused with such old tales. 'Look Tweaky, the earth doesn't exclusively belong to us – the sparrows. Of course, humans will come, the cats will come along with the humans. Who likes the cats anyway? We need to be nice to everyone". My young heart would inexplicably beat faster on hearing the name – cat, I had never seen one though. Even the trespassing wicked humans may have scared my grandpa then. He can't even hear properly now or he would have pulled up Ma for depriving him of spreading such wise explanation. Does everyone get wiser with age? I just hope my Ma would never get old like her Pa, and stays young and chirpy. I hate elderly, aged sparrows, dispensing homilies all the time to obedient little ones like me.

But sometimes it is fun engaging with Grandpa in silly conversations. I would cuddle up to him at dusk,

"When did you come and settle down here in this Champa tree, Grandpa?", I would ask, hiding my poker face from him, whose eyesight had become weaker with age. It didn't matter if I posed this question a hundred times to him. He doesn't mind, he never does; perhaps doesn't remember even, but he loves to jog his memory a bit and unfailingly comes up with this gem –every time!

His voice quivers as he amusingly labours to baby talk to me in a measured tone "O…… I think it was many springs ago. Your Ma had just learnt to fly. The word went around and we all flew in here in small groups by turns. Tweaky, you won't believe, it was so nice here, plenty of food, insects and the river close enough to bathe every day… but then came the humans, building big houses in front of our tree, laying electric cables…"

Ha Ha! The same old trite story that he loved to repeat to anyone, ad nauseam. Poor old grandpa! I loved his baby talk. He thought I would remain a baby sparrow, frozen in time, forever.

The tired grandpa would then adjust his emaciated body in position, on the branch swaying in the gentle breeze.

"Careful now, you shouldn't exert yourself at your age", chirped the caring Tweaky.

"That is mighty respectful of you.", Grandpa paused to rub his beak on the twig sticking out of the branch, "Just look at the boisterous youngsters these days. If I were to fall down from the branch no one will rush to rescue me before the Cat pounces on my hapless body", the wise old grandpa uttered a gospel truth. Oh no, the word 'cat' sent shivers down my body all the way to the tiny tail. What would a cat look like? A big flying vulture or a four-legged walking animal?

When I was about to be born, I didn't look like a sparrow at all. My mother tells me that I was ensconced in an oblong white shell. Can you believe that? I couldn't see anything, just felt my own soft incipient limbs wrapped around my little body. I could imagine and hear my Ma, chirping happily, sitting smugly on my shell. Once it rained hard; very hard and I shivered even inside the shell. She spread her wings real wide to envelop me tightly.

Well, I wasn't alone in the incommodious nest! There were three more of my siblings in other shells, yes, I could feel them as well, wondering what they must be looking like. I didn't know, but she did.

My little body grew bigger and bigger till one day the shell got too small for me. Oof, I felt so claustrophobic inside!

My God… You see I had to break the unyielding shell with my stubby beak. Fragments of the shell fell around me. Ha, Ha! It was so amusing to see it crumble down.

Wow! I saw my siblings around. I could vaguely make out they were all the same, three of them, like me. It took me several days for my eyes to get adjusted to the bright light around me. I had the first real glimpse of Ma. She was vivacious, stately and all-powerful.

We all were comfortable in our nest that probably Ma had built, hidden in the dense foliage of a tree. Pa may have played some part in building it but more about him later. It was a half-spherical basket, with a whole lot of coarse material on the outside such as straw, twigs, paper, leaves, grasses, and other available materials.

The inside was lined with gossamer feathers and ultra-fine grass with the sweet smell of earth drenched in the first rains. Where did Ma bring these from?

None of my business, as long as she brought food for the four of us.

We chirped like crazy, incessantly all at once to draw Ma's attention to get us some food.

My vision was still blurred but I could see Ma as she brought food and just shoved it down my wide-open beak. I instantly gulped it down, to be ready for the next!

"Tweaky, you are too impatient. Why can't you be well-behaved like your brothers and sisters?", She pulled me up once. I couldn't help making a face at her when she wasn't looking.

Oh, I forgot to tell you about this. There was another bigger sparrow with a black band around its neck. It kept flying in and out. Ma loved him so we too loved him.

"He is your Pa, Tweaky", But tell me why don't I have the lovely black band like him? I was too afraid to ask Mom.

A little later I could clearly figure out that our nest was in a tenebrous corner of a big Champa tree (Plumeria) opposite a house built close by the humans. It was too far for my little eyes then but not any longer. My eyes were getting clearer by the day.

Actually, the house was much taller than I could see. Ma told me that the house belonged to a sprightly old man with a luxuriant tuft of grey hair on his head. Hate to say this but unlike my siblings, I was a bit nosy. I tried to raise my head above the rest to see what was going on in the house inside that window. Are all men the same? I must find out.

My Pa – yes, the one with an exquisite black band around his neck – playfully poked me with his large beak, "Not nice to peep into anyone's house, kid". Miffed, I had to retract myself in the huddle. But why? Why was it not nice?

With my vision getting better and better, I often stared at that man, standing with a cup of tea in his hand, early in the morning and straining his ears to catch the song by the birds teetering on an electric cable, not very far from his window.

How I wish I could fly close to him, sit at his window grill and entice him with my own chatter! But I realized he only wanted to watch birds that sang melodiously. When will I sing?

What was he doing in that big house all day? Was there some food in the house for me?

Once he saw me, making me nervous. He picked up something that had two round glasses that he held closely pressed to his eyes, with fervid intensity. Wasn't he peeping into my house now? I blushed and slipped inside the nest. Not fair. I will tell Ma, – not to Pa; too scared of him, Oh yeah!

I made up my mind to learn to sing, from…, Umm, let's see… who else but from Ma, silly!

"I cannot teach you. You have to watch me sing and learn to sing all by yourself", Why, for God's sake? I may be a slow learner but not torpid…

I wanted to make a face again but couldn't. She was my Ma you know? She would know what is right for me.

But how can I observe what goes on in her voice box? I stopped talking to her for a few days. Two of my siblings somehow learnt to fly on their own and simply vanished. The one with a black band around his neck – just like Dad – stayed back; yeah, I was a slow learner, but don't tell anyone ok? Oh, good, so now there was some more room for the two of us in the nest.

You know, Meethu, that parrot with a nice green coat and that funny aquiline beak was a big prankster. He just ate the seeds of the guava and spat out the sweet marrow of the fruit. He would fly in from somewhere, with a big guava fruit in his beak, settle down above our branch and merrily start eating it. The prankster that he is, the soft marrow kept falling over our nest, and he laughed his heart out.

Ma was very angry. Breathing fire, she went right in front of him and scolded him at the top of her voice. Everyone around wondered what had happened to Ma. Meethu never dared to do it again. That is my Ma.

But then I saw Ma crying one day. Pa never came home. She sang even when she cried. I sat close to her and tried to speak to her, lovingly. It was at that moment I realised I could sing as well; I could sing as I spoke to her. The song came out spontaneously, without effort, from deep within.

"Where is Dad? Are you waiting for him?"

"The big vulture grabbed him and flew away, far … away" She sobbed

"Oh, my poor Ma!", I clung to her, "I would never leave you, dear"

Chirpter 2

It took some days for Ma to come to terms with life after the tragedy with Pa. I cosied up to comfort her, singing the songs that Pa loved to hear from Ma. Why did the cunning vulture snatch my Pa away? I was furiously sad but tried hard to put up a brave face for Ma, oh I loved her so much. She barely moved away from me and Joe.

The rest of the flock in the Champa tree didn't care much except for an occasional visit reminding Ma and me to be brave. Meethu, chastened by Ma's outburst turned out to be a much well-behaved bird, often bringing some fruits for us.

My brother Joe was keen to fly off to places far away like Pa. He detested staying put in the nest all day and going on singing, like me.

Sometimes, Joe would get into a depression. He would just sit there and do nothing as if wondering about the dark future ahead. Ma tried her best to cheer him up to no avail. Sometimes he would not look at the food brought by Ma. That wasn't fair. He was my brother. I cuddled up to him and told him, 'Joe, please be nice to Ma. Our Pa isn't going to be back ever.'

"Oh, but why?", he was inconsolable, "Why can't we have our Pa back?"

Ma overheard him. She sighed and flew off. I shivered at the thought of losing both Pa and Ma. Who will fly out and bring food for us now?

Then one day we saw her, not Ma, but a huge black cat stealthily climbing up the tree, purring menacingly. We could clearly see her whiskers as she closed in.

One two three, both of us, shell shocked, raised an alert, help, help!

The man in that house got up and looked at us from his window. I had nearly forgotten all about that man in the house across the tree. As soon as he saw the cat getting closer, he clapped loudly to scare the cat away. That didn't work. He picked up some heavy bundle lying in the house and threw it at the cat, yelling to scare the predator away.

Mercifully, it worked. The cat hesitated and quickly retreated, jumped down to the ground and disappeared among the bushes.

He smiled as he saw our Ma flying back to protect us.

"Oh Ma, where were you?"

"Don't worry, kids. It is time you learn to fly now"

Did the man ever know about the ghastly tragedy about our Pa? I bet he wasn't aware of my newly found skill of singing like the other birds swaying on that electric wire. Or he would have trained his binoculars on the tree to seek me out.

But why was I so obsessed with the man? Not easy to answer at all. Why should he care if I sing at all? Again, not easy. Don't ask me.

I know. He not only loved to listen to the singing birds but to see them as well. They were birds of all hues, but not sparrows, like me.

Did he care for their beauty or the songs? Perhaps both. I can't be charming like other exotic birds. I can only sing. Why am I not beautiful like a peacock? The peacocks can't sing.

But I am sure he did care about me. When will I look beautiful as well? Ma says the sparrows cannot look as beautiful as peacocks.

The flying lessons started the same day in the right earnest.

I told you I was a slow learner but my brother Joe was quick. He took to flying like the fish takes to water. Ma had a close look at my little body. My wings had not developed fully yet. I tried hard but they wouldn't open fully. It was so exasperating. Now the responsibility of protecting me from the predators fell on my brother whenever Ma was away in search of food.

Oh no! I was so keen to learn how to fly. I wanted to fly to that window, sit on the grill and sing for that man who was like an angel to us. Didn't he save us from that scary cat? What will he think of us? That sparrows have no etiquette?

Brother Joe could fly but not sing. Ma was too busy. I didn't want to be an uncouth sparrow. Sometimes I heard strange but divine music from the house. I tried my best to sing along but my weak voice got drowned in the noises around the tree. Was he the one singing in the house? Or playing some instrument? I must find out soon.

It was springtime now. Cuckoo, the bird with the most melodious voice, filled the area with divine songs, as sweet as the sugar. It was so amusing to see the man jump and rush to the window to listen to the cuckoo. Once he even opened the grill of the window to look at her, singing like a queen. I watched him for the first time without the grill blocking the view. He had two big eyes, somewhat brownish, and had some wrinkles on his large forehead that showed up as sharp creases whenever he was looking at something in rapt attention.

Why couldn't I sing like a cuckoo? I will ask Ma when she returns.

"You can never sing like the cuckoo, stupid", Joe teased me.

"Why? What makes you say that?", I didn't like his negative attitude. He is so mean!

"Simple, you are not a cuckoo, that is why. Ha Ha Ha"

"Shut up, will you? One day, I will sing better than the Cuckoo. Just watch"

"You cannot even fly"

"He ha ha, is that an argument? Stop teasing", I just shut him up. Poor Joe!

I wanted to sing as well as the Cuckoo, why, even better. Can I ask that gracious man to teach me? Crazy thoughts! I do not even know him. But what melodious tunes he creates every day that haunts me in my dreams! I want to sing for him at the window. How stupid of me! I must be able to fly first. Joe is not wrong after all. Shouldn't have rubbed him the wrong way. I am sure I will fly one day, soon. Does the man have a listening device to listen to my songs from here, like he does to see something from a distance? I don't need to fly there!

Ma always takes my side in any verbal duel with Joe. Would Pa have taken Joe's side? One day, Joe will fly off on his own, uh uh, not like Pa. Pa was grabbed by that big bird. The cunning vulture would have dropped Pa back, only if he had heard Ma cry out in anguish!

It was springtime. The migrant phoebes started returning from their winter homes of the north, with their tail bobbing near the edge of the garden that humans had built. They got busy building their nests on the ledges jutting out of the walls of the building.

They somehow love being close to the humans. Woodpeckers couldn't be far behind. A lone male woodpecker got amorously close to his lady love, trying to feed her, fluffing his feathers and ended up with a courtship dance.

Ma now brings insects and spiders for our meals, not the bland seeds of wheat grains and weeds. The tree was laden with bountiful Champa flowers.

Love was in the air. Ma looked refreshingly happy now, I didn't have the courage to ask her why. She is my Ma. Let her be happy. You don't need a reason to be happy but who knows? Could it be the cupid?

But soon the secret was out. She returned with another male sparrow. Spectacular, fatherly figure! Together they flew in, singing love songs that I had never heard before. My brother joined me in welcoming them.

'Joe, look, Ma is happy again'. Tears of joy trickled down my face. Joe looked heavenward 'Oh my God, she sure does!' Happy days were here again.

I turned my head instinctively at the window. A divine music was wafting our way from there. Was it that man? My man? Oh man, come out and see the joy in Ma's eyes. I can then see you.

Ma told my new Pa to teach me to fly. He smiled, "Come on Tweaky, it's easy. Just let yourself go"

"But the wings don't open up and my little body will plummet all the way to the ground"

"They will open, they have to, take my word for it"

"Ok, but first I will try to fly to that window, just watch me"

Ma was looking with bated breath, 'Yes, my dear, you certainly can, go!'

I took off hastily and promptly fell to the ground. Luckily it was not a major fall. Pa flew over and comforted me, "It happens Tweaky, it happened to me, it happens to all of us"

"But…"

"Just try again", the look in Ma's eyes said it all, no fussing over her darling Tweaky. Joe's mischievous eyes said it all 'I told you'.

Right then I saw the man opening the window grill. He smiled. I was in awe of the man, awash with a feeling I never had known.

I must try now, for him; my man is watching! He will teach me to sing like the Cuckoo. It was as if my whole body danced with excitement. Fly baby, fly.

There was no fall this time. Ma and Pa chirped with joy. The lazy Joe didn't stir at all from his slumber.

I landed safely at the window grill and chirped back at Ma and Pa.

Ma looked a bit worried seeing me settled on the window. How to trust a stranger? A man?

The man took some steps back from the window and watched me in amazement from the centre of his room. I turned and signalled the happy parents that I was ok. Pa flew off on his survey mission.

I entered the house from the window. Had never seen such a big room. It really was a spacious room. There were huge sofa sets arranged in front of a TV set. A beautiful dining table in one corner ready with some plates and spoons laid out.

But who are these people in the photographs? His family?

I flew further inside and sat on the dining table and then hopped onto the sofa set and then out of the main entrance where I saw his name – Raj – on a nameplate. Easy!

So, it was the family of my dream man Raj in the pictures. But it is not nice to ask too many personal questions right in the first meeting – my first Pa had advised me. Bless his soul.

Raj was amused to no end at my moves in the room. He took out his mobile phone and tried to take a video but I kept flying around with agility now. The phone almost slipped off from his hands. No wonder it was hard for him.

Arey baba, I will keep flying in and out, now that I have spread my wings. Don't be so impatient capturing me in flight!

Raj seemed to understand my thought process. He put his phone aside.

Wait, how is this guy going to teach me to sing like a cuckoo? Aha, it must be the music from the TV program! No, it can't be. I distinctly recall his singing some tunes for long hours.

He realised I must be hungry. He emptied some grains from a jar in an open dish for me and stepped back to see if I had eaten. I told you my man could read my thoughts, didn't I?

The grains were so good I finished everything he had laid out for me! Had never tasted such mouth-watering grains in my life. It seemed I ate more than I should have. Inevitable! My stomach started hurting. For a while, I felt miserable. Or was it an attempt to seek his attention? He felt guilty. Did he offer something I shouldn't have eaten? I really wanted Raj to get closer and caress my head with his manly hand. I shut my eyes in anticipation…

Ma called me out from the tree.

"Dinner time, Tweaky, fly home now. Pa will be back soon"

I wasn't hungry at all but had to fly home.

What about that music? Maybe, find out tomorrow. And about the faces in the photographs – tomorrow?

He saw me flying back to the nest all the way, waving bye.

Ma was very happy about my new friendship with that man – Raj.

"Be careful, Tweaky. Always on your guard"

"Not to worry, Ma. Wanted to say "I will sing like a cuckoo soon"; but not today. She might think I am crazy. I fell asleep, dreaming of Raj. What an obsession with the man? Shake it off, Tweaky. He can't chirp like you, can't fly like the sparrows.

Chirpter 3

I wanted to fly back to that window; to Raj's window in the morning. Recurring dreams of me flying off to distant hills. With Raj? Funny dreams! Raj flying? But he sings, every day. I will sing like a cuckoo one day and Raj will fly like me, one day.

Once I begin flying confidently Raj will learn to fly from me. He will teach me how to sing then.

But it started raining at night. Rains? In winter? Ma said it happened sometimes.

My frail body shivered in the cold winds that swept across the sugarcane field. The rustling of the leaves made dreadful noises. I crept close to Ma and slept.

When I woke up the next morning it was still raining heavily. The rainwater collected on the leaves and pitter-pattered as big drops, making musical sounds as they fell on the ground below, covered with fallen leaves. The sun hadn't come out yet. How would I fly today? Ma said it was all right to skip flying for a day, no need to show off. Your soft wings will get wet. Hold it, Tweaky! Ma was always too indulgent to me, I felt.

I looked at the window across my nest. It was still shut. Hadn't Raj woken up yet? Did he feel the cold air? I was lucky to snuggle close to Ma but Raj? But poor Raj! He had no one in his house, except those pictures. Then who is he singing for? For himself? He is fond of listening to the birds sing. Will he listen to my song when I sing? Oh Tweaky, you're overthinking. Hold it Tweaky, no point in flying to the window.

"I have to go, Tweaky. Now behave yourself, Ok?' Ma nearly yelled at me, 'Just stay put in the nest. I will be back soon." She flew off to get some food for me, after circling around the tree, she always did that ritual, may be to make sure everything around me was safe.

Where were Pa and my brother, Joe. Was Ma the only one worried about me? I know Joe didn't care much but Pa? May be, he is too busy. I really do not know what the male sparrows did all day?

The nest was getting too small for me now. I crept out of the nest carefully and settled on the curvaceous little branch where the Champa flowers swayed in the air. I could now clearly see that there was another nest down below my branch. There were only three chicks in there. Is that all? How stupid of me! All the nests may not have four chicks. It was so funny the way they looked. Is that the way I would have looked then? Hope not! I think I saw a mirror in Raj's big room. Must peep in there and check out how I look now.

My feathers aren't great, unlike the peacock I saw the other day. The peacock looked splendid with those long flowing feathers. But they weigh him down; the peacock can barely fly a few feet above the ground.

My feathers are lousy. But I can fly high up there in the sky. Tweaky, Tweaky, Tweaky, calm down. You are obsessed with good looks like a peacock, you want to fly like your Pa and sing like a cuckoo! Are you trying to entice someone? Maybe that man? ...

It stopped raining. I was ravenously hungry. Suddenly I saw the window opening with a loud bang. It was the wind that made it hard for Raj to keep the window in place. I saw him bolt it securely.

But what had happened to Raj? He looked dishevelled, his hair fluttering in the wind.

His figure was now fully visible in the window. He yawned, looked up at the sky and smiled. I chirped to draw his attention but he didn't notice me. He ignored me, perhaps the wind whistling through the window muffled my chirp.

A strange desire to get close to him overpowered my senses but it was too scary to fly up there without Ma looking over from here. What if I fall? The mother sparrow of the chicks in the nest below returned with large chunks of meal for them. My stomach protested. Why was my Ma not back yet? I was starving.

Let me risk flying out to him. I can be with him and if I am lucky, he will feed me as well. But as soon as I took the plunge, he shut the window up again. I landed safely outside the window and started knocking on the window pane with my beak, 'Open up Raj, look who is here? I am hungry. Won't you feed me?'

The window remained shut. The wind got calmer now. I could hear the sound of some heavenly music from the house.

'Stop knocking, Tweaky, will you?' I told myself.

I forgot all about my being hungry. The music was so soothing I could sit there all day and keep listening. He was not singing. He was playing some instrument. I hoped he would not stop the music, even to open the window for me.

Just then, "Tweaky, come and have your breakfast", Ma was back.

'Shhhhhhh……, I shook my head vigorously.

'But the window is shut. It is too cold for you; your friend won't open it any time soon.', How would Ma know that I had been listening to some music?

Tweaky! Behave yourself? Come back, right now

I gave up in exasperation. For Ma, the worldly pangs of hunger meant more. I couldn't see him but tasted his music.

"Why can't you eat slowly, for once, Tweaky?" Ma saw me devouring the insects she had brought for me. Just then I saw a beautiful peacock flying past the Champa tree, making a strange guttural sound. He was flying low dragging his weighty feathers along the flight path. Didn't he look stunning?

'Ma, why am I so tiny and not as beautiful as that peacock?'

'Sis, you are a tiny spa......rrow, and can never be as beautiful as that peacock', it was that mischievous Joe taunting me again.

'Shut up, will you?' Ma was quick to reprimand him, 'You are as beautiful as you think, Tweaky, but do you want to be happy as a sparrow or while away your time in trying to be a peacock; in trying to sing like a cuckoo?'

"But why?"

"Ask your Pa". That was her ploy to get off any silly, interminable conversation.

Very clever you are, Ma. All mothers always have a way to deal with their children.

I will get into the house and watch myself in the huge mirror that I saw that day, I promised myself. Maybe I could use some of that stuff in the bottles lying next to the mirror and have a makeover. But I won't tell Ma about it. I want to see the surprised expression on her face when she sees me after the makeover. I will look as beautiful as that peacock.

She can't stop me from singing like a cuckoo, Raj will teach me. There he was in the afternoon! He looked as fresh as ever, with an enigmatic smile on his face. Did he approve of my eavesdropping on his music in the morning?

Here is a secret! I saw Ma and Pa busy in some strange ritual, away from the nest. It was funny the way they snuggled close to each other, very close indeed, picking up some ticks from each other's bodies and then looking at each other, ending up by locking their beaks together when no one was looking, finally hiding in the thick foliage behind. It was a bit funny but I didn't care. It made it easy for me to sneak out again, to that window again.

It was a bit warm in the day. The window was open. I peeped in. There was no one in the main room. There was no music either. Where was Raj? I entered the room, looked around and settled on one of the blades of the ceiling fan that started rotating slowly the moment I sat on it. Circling around, I surveyed the room.

There were picture frames neatly set up just below the TV set. The biggest picture showed a woman with an enigmatic smile on her face. Who was she? She did look familiar. I have no clue why. Her quivering lips were trying to say something to me.

Then there were other people in the frames next to it. They all looked happy, Raj was flanked by his two young girls, a young family with two other little girls playfully posing for the picture. Everything appeared so familiar to me.

I turned my attention to the picture of the woman.

There was something in the smile of the woman that was familiar. Had I seen her somewhere? She looked so endearing! Oh, the mirror was right there on the opposite wall! I turned my head and tried to look at my own reflection in the mirror.

But where was I? There was no Tweaky in the mirror! I just saw exactly the same woman smiling at me from the mirror. Where is Tweaky? Why can't I see myself in the mirror? I turned again and looked at the woman. Her smile had grown even wider. Was she trying to tell me something? I turned around once more and looked into the mirror. There she was, looking back at me from the mirror! It was as if I was that woman and the woman was looking into the mirror!

I was breathless! How could that be? The mirror showed me up as that woman.

The door of the bedroom opened. Raj emerged into the living room and looked at me, puzzled. Was he looking at me as if I was that woman? He looked into the mirror and back to me. Did he see me in the mirror? Or only that woman? He rushed towards me. I got scared and hastily flew back towards the open window.

He stopped for a moment, looked at the picture and me in disbelief. What was wrong?

I saw him slumped on the floor, sobbing unabashedly.

Poor Raj! What had happened? I just couldn't take it anymore and hastily flew back to my nest. The window remained open for a long time. Raj wouldn't appear at the window, perhaps never? Don't know why but I longed to see him. Was he all right? Did he hurt himself? There was no one in the house to look after him. Should I fly back and comfort him?

Chirpter 4

Sleep evaded me that night. The rains too came lashing at everything. I came out of the nest as it fell crashing to the ground. I didn't care; I didn't need it anymore. My mind was filled with hundreds of doubts, about my identity. Who was I anyway? I prayed for the rains to stop, so I could fly there and break through the window and check on Raj. Was he able to sleep at all? It was too painful for me to see Raj slumped on the floor and weeping on seeing me.

Deep inside me some human soul stirred up. Did he see someone else in me? Was that the woman he loved? And lost her somehow? I don't want to see him in pain. He should not see me, ever. I better not go near him. But how can I not see him? I love him so much. It was as if the darkness of the night had enveloped my soul. I want his music, want to feel him, want to see him. A lone owl hooted somewhere close. Its call unnerved me.

The long shoots of sugarcane swayed menacingly in the wind, making an eerie sound. Far away, some villagers were dancing to scary drumbeats. Oh my God, help!

Was that mirror cursed? Or was it a magic mirror? Am I responsible for the pain on his face? I was torn between the two worlds – that of the human and that of a sparrow. The more I thought the clearer it was that the mirror was the cause. Yes, it was that mirror. Go Tweaky and knock that mirror down with your beak. Go Tweaky, go. At last, my mind was at rest with that resolve. The rains too subsided to a light drizzle in solidarity. It lulled me to sleep.

In my dream, I saw my beak shatter the mirror into pieces, my beak bleeding profusely. But I had taken my revenge. The mirror deserved it. Raj came running over, and picked me up lovingly in his hands, caressing my frail body gently. I turned to look at the woman in the photo but the photo was blank. There was no woman in there! What had happened to her? I mean, her photo? I wanted to see me in that mirror, see her again but the mirror lay in pieces now, all because of you, Tweaky. You are selfish, Tweaky. Yes, you are. Would that make Raj sad again?

'Wake up, Tweaky. What happened to your beak? My goodness, it is swollen', Ma was staring at my beak. Oh, did I knock the branch of the tree with my beak in my dream?

'It's nothing Ma. I will be all right', I evaded her searching eyes.

'Hmm, do you want to fly out with me to catch some food today?'

Was that a question or a gentle command?

I moved my head to look at the window but the movement hurt my neck. The window was open, even the grill.

'Tweaky, did you hear me?', now Ma's voice was a real command, 'come on, grow up. I can't go on feeding you all your life'

But what was my life? Was it my life? Am I a sparrow? Or that woman? Wasn't my life there with Raj, in that spacious house? What will happen to my longing to be beautiful like the beautiful peacock? To sing like a cuckoo? When? How? Even Ma cannot answer these questions. She had all the answers to my naive questions till then but not anymore. I had grown up in the course of one dark night.

'Yes, Ma, happy to join you for the adventure'

But what if I can't fly far enough to catch an insect all by myself? But what if the mirror stayed intact and the woman stays in that photo? I must find out.

I threw a final glance at the window as we flew past. He was nowhere to be seen. Where was he?

I nearly missed hitting a branch hanging low.

'Careful, my child, you must watch out when you fly out here in the open'

'Yes Ma, I can't afford to aggravate the injury anyway', I tried to smile but the scar in my little heart burned like a red hot coal. There was no respite from the train of thoughts that kept coming at me. Will he be there when we return in the evening? I went through the motions of catching some insects and got some grains. The training lasted a couple of weeks. Still no trace of Raj. Was he all right? That woman we saw in the mirror must have now emerged out of the broken mirror and must be looking after Raj.

I was certain Ma would have known everything that happened to me, that I lied about the injury and my stealing glances at the window all the time. But it was all a question of feeling each other out, without the spoken word. Ma and I had mastered it by now.

That evening I got the shock of my life. I saw him. But there was another woman with him in his car as he drove into the building. She looked attractive enough but nowhere near that lovely woman in the photo. Who was that? But why am I jealous? Who am I?

My heart sank. He doesn't care for me. Did he consider me responsible for that mirror episode? I had nothing to do with it. It was that woman in the photo who played some magic trick. And what is he doing with that new woman?

I resented going on the food mission with Ma. Enough of learning, Ma. I can manage now. I had grown up. Do I still want to sing like a cuckoo? Do I still want to look like a peacock? Or...... look like that lovely woman? I hate being a sparrow. I hate that other woman. I hate my Ma. I hate everything and everyone around.

Tweaky, you long to be the woman in the photo, don't you?

I sensed a strange yearning in my heart now. Was that a sign of growing up? Ma watched me over and smiled mischievously at times. How would Raj react to my new avatar? What do I care? Let him be with that new woman.

What was Raj doing all day anyway? He rarely ever appeared at the window. I don't care.

I flew off one day, all by myself, leaving Ma confused and worried. Let her worry. Let Raj worry if he cares for me at all. I just wanted to get away from it all, fly off far away where even Ma never ventured.

But I will return for sure, to see Raj's reaction to my new avatar, see him flustered and apologetic for not caring for me. That will teach him a lesson. How about kneeling before me and asking for a pardon? Hmmm, I will pardon him, no I won't.

I tried to forget everything and just kept flying, as I made my way over the open fields of sugarcane, rice fields, ponds, and rivers. I sang as I flew but not as well as the cuckoo. A flock of other birds flew in formation just above me. Lovely. The sparrows don't fly that high. The sadness that had gripped me disappeared slowly to welcome a new life, that of expectations, and new friends.

I longed for a nice handsome male sparrow, to fly together, singing new songs, locking our beaks together – just like Ma and Pa. My little heart beat faster and faster in anticipation of the new life.

Yes, that's what I will do. Find a new friend, fly back together to that Champa tree and make that Raj jealous. If he can find someone to fill the void, so can I.

'It's madness, Tweaky' – my inner voice warned me, 'you will ruin everything.'

I don't care. He has to pay for all the pain I have suffered. He will.

I flew around a cluster of houses next to a hillock and sat down on the branch of a tree. There were all kinds of birds but no sparrows. Oh, but wait. There was one. It was a fully grown male sparrow, looking disdainfully at me. What did he think of himself? A peacock?

'Hello there? What happened to your beak? Did you dip it in some red cherry sauce? Ha Ha Ha'

I hated his making fun of my beak. I straightened up and looked directly at him.

"I am Tweaky and my red-hot beak can bite. Who are you, some local mafia king?'

'Wow! What an attitude?'

He crept closer, walking with a swagger, rubbed his beak sideways on a branch of the tree and said,' My Pa calls me Zap', without taking his eyes off me.

'Zap! What a funny name! Ha Ha Ha', I mimicked his style.

'Maybe, but that's my name. But I like your name, Tweaky. Looking great too.'

Interesting! I couldn't help repeating his routine of rubbing my beak.

'Where are you from?', I must admit the guy looked fascinating.

'I am from a faraway place; I bet you cannot fly that far'

'And what makes you say that?', he crept closer. My heart beat faster.

Zap was arguably very handsome. The wooing game had begun.

'Aha, look who is challenging the macho sparrow, like me?'

I danced around him instinctively.

"Does the macho Zap accept the challenge or just sit here all day and rub his beak endlessly?'

Now there was no looking back. He came even closer and planted a kiss on my beak. I couldn't protest. His smell was overpowering, his smile, cute. That was a macho kiss, very adventurous of him. I loved his boldness. It felt really good beyond my wildest imagination. I kissed him back, with my wings fluttering like crazy. I could see his full body as he opened his wings wide apart, exposing a prominent red mark on the left side of his face.

'What is this red mark, Zap'

'Oh, that is my birthmark. You won't lose me that way!' He laughed heartily. My mind went crazy with delight. For a moment, I forgot all my sorrows, even Raj. Nothing mattered any more, except my determination to take revenge.

'Come, let us fly together back to my place. You will love it'

The fire in my heart was still burning bright. I must go and show my prized catch and make Raj go green with envy. First thing first, the romance with Zap can wait.

We flew together, crossing beautiful fields. Huge green trees welcomed us; the flowers smiled at us. We sang all the way back to the Champa tree, my home.

'Look Zap, that is where we are going', I pointed in the direction of my home as we came closer. Going home! I flew faster and faster, leaving Zap behind, panting.

Right at the window, Raj was looking out. Was he looking for me? Poor man! He saw me flying past and waved at me. I think I saw a puzzled expression on his face and I know exactly why.

'Who is that man, waving at you, Tweaky?' Zap's curiosity had nothing to do with jealousy. How would he ever know about Raj?

I ignored Zap's question and both of us flew into our home. Ma welcomed us warmly, watching Zap mischievously.

Raj shut the window with a big bang. That's it. Happy now? I knew why he was angry. He deserves that. Where was he hiding all these days? Go and make merry with your woman.

Honestly, I hoped the new woman wouldn't be there now, that Raj would wait for me to fly in his room, that he would wish Zap to get lost.

I would wait till tomorrow for the spring to burst into a thousand flowers. Hope the mirror was still there. And when I look into the mirror the lovely woman would appear again.

Ma got busy preparing for dinner.

Chirpter 5

There was a nip in the air at night but my mind furiously was at work, to confront Raj next morning. Pity the poor Zap. I had no real desire to trap him to get at Raj. He is cocky but nice to befriend. He was sleeping on the next branch, tired of the long light, and oblivious of the drama to unfold the next day.

The rustle of the leaves sounded like a harp playing a romantic number, or was it Raj playing some magic music on his instrument? The Champa flowers around bloomed spectacularly in the full moon sailing in the sky. This could be a perfect set-up for my reunion with Raj, provided Destiny did not play some dirty trick once again. What about that new scheming woman? That's easy, once Raj sees me, she will fly the coop.

The enchanting music made me restive. How I wanted someone to cuddle me up, like the other night when he lovingly held me in his palm, caressing me, feeling sorry for my bleeding beak?

I let out a big scream with pleasure at the sensation of his palm wrapping around me – Zap stirred a bit but went back to his sleep. He would have asked me all uncomfortable questions. Why would I like to reveal my secret? This poor creature is just a ploy for my path to happiness. Once I am on my way, he can fly back to wherever he came from. I smiled like a scheming villain but no one noticed it.

I longed for more of the vicarious titillations lasting through the long night. Zap woke up at the stroke of dawn, refreshed and huggable but did I care? I rubbed my beak on the slender branch hanging next to him. He thought it was a courting ritual! Stupid Zap!

Good, my secrets will remain secrets. Ma watched me flirting with Zap, visibly happy and relieved. She too had no inkling of what was coming my way. Her Tweaky, the Eve in the Garden of Eden, was ready to eat the forbidden apple, but this was not it. Everything is fair in love and…

Zap's half-open dreamy eyes held no interest for me.

'Who was that man at the window, waving at us yesterday?', Zap asked again, innocently.

Was he getting jealous?

'Oh, just a friend who feeds me exotic grains. Want to come along with me?' I countered with a facade of innocence. How would the poor Zap ever understand my overtures?

'Well, I do not mind, if you come along', Zap was getting into deeper trouble.

Hey Tweaky, have you ever thought of Raj ditching you and Zap flying away in a huff for cheating on him? No way. The thought of the wide brown eyes of Raj playing the magical music egged me on.

The sun rose magnificently. Cock-a-doodle-doo – announced the rooster. I took a deep breath as the window opened with a bang. He's calling me, go Tweaky go. I made a dash for my dream man, Zap followed me.

There he was, smiling at me, playing magical music! The lovely woman with quivering lips was in the photo. Zap and I flew in and stood together. But the moment I looked at the mirror opposite the photo, she disappeared from the photo frame, smiling in the reflection, standing beside Zap! Where was my reflection in the mirror? Scared, I looked around. No Tweaky in the reflection! What was Zap doing standing next to the lovely woman in the reflection? It was so surreal!

Raj walked up to the woman in the photo – I could see Raj through the mirror, but not in the photo.

Did Zap see anything? He appeared dazed. He looked in the mirror but where was Tweaky? Not seen in the reflection! Zap didn't find Tweaky in the reflection.

It didn't matter what was happening in the room. What mattered was happening in the reflection in the mirror!

The mirror showed Raj standing next to the woman. Oh, but in reality, he was standing next to me! Even Zap saw this weird scene. For him, Tweaky mattered the most. Where was she in the mirror? In a moment of utter confusion, he flew aggressively towards the mirror and dashed against it, hoping to find me. The impact hurled him down to the floor.

Raj lifted Zap up and stared at him, both appeared to be in a state of a trance. The woman in the reflection opened her arms to welcome.

In the very next moment, the mirror came crashing down, breaking into hundreds of pieces falling all around Raj and Zap!

It was incredible whatever was happening around. The cool blast of breeze from the window made the tiny pieces of broken glass rise in a swirling motion. I closed my eyes. It was impossible to see anything clearly.

When I opened my eyes, I saw Raj and Zap rising from the cloud of swirling broken glass. The mirror was totally shattered and gone. It wasn't there! There was no woman either! Where was she? I felt she was right inside me; her soul was my soul now. The lovely woman was me, Tweaky now.

I saw Raj walking towards me but strangely, his gait had changed. He had a red mark on his left cheek! This was no Raj that I had known!

Zap got up and hopped back towards me. His eyes were brown and the red mark on his face was gone! That was Raj, in the body of Zap. He sat down beside me.

Miracle! Zap was no Zap. He was my Raj, in the form of sparrow!

Raj, with a red mark on his left cheek, wearily settled down on the chair, looking dazed.

'Let us go Tweaky', Zap beckoned me. I had one last look at the human Raj and joined Zap on the way out. His brown eyes had the same magic that Raj had.

The sugar canes dancing in the spring weather welcomed us. Ma looked at us and bade us goodbye.

Together, we flew to distant rivers, and hills – untiring, singing songs that Raj used to play. My whole little body danced with joy, I sang like a Cuckoo, with goosebumps that I had never felt. Love makes one sing like a cuckoo.

'Ma, look I am singing like a cuckoo, see, I promised you', but she was not with us.

It was magic. Raj and I belonged to a different world, blissful and heavenly.

As we flew low over green fields and tiny villages, little children watched us and exclaimed, 'Look there goes a pair of birds more beautiful than the peacock! I looked at Raj flying next to me, 'Hey Raj, we are more beautiful than the peacock!'

'Sure,' he smiled back. 'Love does transform sparrows into peacocks'

'Look Ma, I am a beautiful bird like the peacock, didn't I promise you?' She wasn't there with us to see that either.

I had no idea how far we had flown together in bliss, with my eternal companion, my soulmate. It looked as if we circled the world over till that Champa tree appeared again.

'Look, Raj, there is that Champa tree', I cried out in excitement.

And that window? Did Zap still live there, in the form of a human? I flew inside the house through the window that was ajar. Again, it was a full moon night. There was no one in the house. The mirror was gone. There was no sign of life. Where was he?

I was scared now, all alone in that haunted house. What if the window shuts itself on its own, locking me in the house, forever?

I looked around. A dazzling bright beam of the full moon shone over the face of that lovely woman in the photo. Someone had garlanded the photo with flowers that had withered long ago. The garland extended to another photo next to her. I saw Raj in the photo, with a red mark on his left cheek, and a faint smile on his face.

Epilogue

That full moon night, Tweaky sneaked into Raj's room to find his photo, garlanded along with that of the lovely woman. Some withered flowers of the garland, carefully sewn together by someone, had fallen off, next to the heap of ashes of the incense. The lively frame of her Raj, which she had craved for, was now reduced to a two-dimensional photo, set up on that desk. What was she to make of the vermillion mark on his forehead identical to that on the woman's forehead?

'I can't take it, Raj', she cried out. Her anguished cry echoed across the empty room.

Wait, who is strumming the heavenly instrument? Oh, it is so dark around here.

The window cracked open and a strong breeze rushed in. Startled, Tweaky turned her head slowly, in the direction of the window.

'What is Zap doing outside the window?' She saw Zap in suspended animation, his wings flapping like a bee, except that there was no buzzing noise. Scary! She thought her heart missed a beat, Zap flapping like a bee outside the window, unable to come in, unwilling to disappear out of sight.

The mysterious strumming sound grew louder by the minute. It was coming from a corner in the room, sounding like coming from deep inside a cave.

'Just come in Zap, I can't take it any more', She found she was sinking, next to the photo of that lovely woman. Zap didn't even look at her and kept flapping his wings outside the window. There was no mirror. But she thought she saw her reflection at the top of the desk.

As she sank into the solid desk, the vermillion mark from the foreheads of Raj and that woman fell off and the garland flew off, out of the window, pushing out Zap to oblivion. The strumming grew louder and louder, Tweaky shut her eyes, unable to comprehend the mystery unfolding.

The huge clock on the wall struck midnight. There was no one to witness the miracle. There was no one there, no photos, no mirror, no Tweaky, no Zap.

Nothing but dead silence. Everyone had attained nirvana.